ADVENTURE AGAINST
THE
ENDERMEN

ADVENTURE AGAINST THE ENDERMEN

AN UNOFFICIAL OVERWORLD HEROES ADVENTURE, BOOK ONE

DANICA DAVIDSON

Sky Pony Press
New York

Sky Pony Press books may be purchased in bulk at special discounts for sales promotion, corporate gifts, fund-raising, or educational purposes. Special editions can also be created to specifications. For details, contact the Special Sales Department, Sky Pony Press, 307 West 36th Street, 11th Floor, New York, NY 10018 or info@skyhorsepublishing.com.

Sky Pony® is a registered trademark of Skyhorse Publishing, Inc.®, a Delaware corporation.

Minecraft® is a registered trademark of Notch Development AB.
The Minecraft game is copyright © Mojang AB.

Visit our website at www.skyponypress.com.

10 9 8 7 6 5 4 3 2 1

Library of Congress Cataloging-in-Publication Data is available on file.

Cover design by Brian Peterson
Cover photo by Lordwhitebear

Paperback ISBN: 978-1-5107-2702-1
Ebook ISBN: 978-1-5107-2708-3

Printed in Canada

ADVENTURE AGAINST THE
THE
ENDERMEN

CHAPTER 1

THE SECOND THAT I STEPPED INTO THE DARK cave, I wanted to get out. It was so black and creepy in there, like the perfect area for monsters to live.

"Scared, Stevie?" one of the village boys mocked me.

I took a deep gulp and looked back over my shoulder. About ten village kids had followed me to the cave. They'd put a couple torches along the cave's walls, though it was still hard to see in there.

"I'm not scared," I said. But I knew my voice didn't sound so confident.

It was my own fault I was in this situation. My dad had wanted to trade supplies with the blacksmith, so I'd followed him to the village and then asked if I could do my own thing. While Dad was taking care of business, I'd searched for some village kids to hang out with. None of the village kids had wanted to be my friend before, but this time I was hoping things would be different.

I had friends, even though they mostly lived on Earth, which was a completely different world. Wouldn't it be nice to have friends right in my own nearby village in the Overworld?

I had started out by talking big. I reminded the kids that I was the one and only Stevie. I was the one who had stopped the zombie takeover of the Overworld. I had defeated Herobrine, the worst monster—or mob, as we called them—our world had ever seen. I had even overcome a Herobrine-created Wither a few weeks before. So I was worth being friends with, right?

At first the kids got really into my story. One kid even said that I was the biggest hero in the Overworld right now. I liked the sound of it. Then one boy said, "We should take him to the cave."

"Cave?" I'd repeated. "What are you talking about?"

"During the Wither attack, the Wither blasted open a mountain by the village and there's this huge cave inside," the boy said. "There's a big hole near the entrance of the cave and we've been daring one another to jump over it. No one's been brave enough to."

"A hole?" I said. Jumping over a hole didn't sound too bad.

"You can do it, Stevie!" a village girl shouted. It was the one who'd said I was a hero. "It'll be easy for you!"

Everyone was looking at me expectantly. So, of course I said, "Show me the cave!"

It wasn't until I agreed that I realized I probably should have gotten more information first. Dad had told me a million times not to run into things without understanding the situation.

When we reached the cave, I saw just how big and dark it was. It didn't matter that it was sunny outside, because the cave was shady enough for mobs like creepers or zombies or armed skeletons to be walking around inside. I had my diamond sword and my toolkit with me, and I held them close.

The boy who'd come up with the idea of going to the cave—the same boy who'd asked me if I was scared—showed me where the hole was. It was close to the cave entrance, so at least I didn't have to go far into the cave. But it was a much larger hole than I realized. It was more than just a missing block or two out of the ground.

I pulled a torch out of my toolkit so I could see better. When I knelt down and waved the torch into the hole, I still couldn't even see the bottom. Not a good sign.

"What's wrong?" the boy mocked. When I lifted the torch back up, the flames made his teasing smile look spooky. There was just something so cruel about the way he grinned at me. "This is nothing compared to what you've done before, is it? Or is a little hole in the ground too scary for Stevie?"

I was starting to remember why I wasn't friends with the village kids. But when I stood up and looked back over them, I saw how closely they were watching me. If I didn't jump over the hole, they'd all think I was a wimp. On top of that, they'd think I was a liar. And I definitely wouldn't be called a "hero" anymore.

I examined the hole, trying to figure out if I even could jump over it. It was possible, though it'd be a stretch. I suddenly wondered where Dad was. It'd be great if he could show up to say he was done seeing the blacksmith and it was time to go home. That would give me an excuse to leave, but Dad didn't even know where I was.

"I think the rumor is true," the mocking boy said in a loud voice. "Stevie didn't really defeat any of those mobs. He was there, but I bet his dad took care of all the work. And then he *acts* like he's the Overworld's hero."

Some kids whispered in agreement. I couldn't take it anymore—I jumped up, riled. I'd spent my whole life living in my dad's shadow. His name was Steve, and everyone knew him as The Steve because how good he was at building and fighting mobs. But I'd worked hard in my recent battles, even saving Dad a few times. I deserved the credit! (And I didn't want to think about the fact I was just hoping Dad would swoop in and save me.)

"Here, take my sword and my torch," I said gruffly, pushing the objects into the mocking boy's hands. I didn't need them messing up my balance. Now I just had my toolkit slung over my shoulder, but I was used to moving around with that.

The boy took my sword and torch, surprised. That made me feel a little better, because I realized he'd been expecting me to chicken out.

I walked back a bit so I could get a really good running start. I eyed the hole like an enemy I had to defeat.

Get ready, Stevie, I told myself. *You can do this!*

The next thing I knew, I was running. The kids were all cheering, except for the mocking boy, who looked disappointed. Shadows from the cave were coming up all around me as the hole kept getting closer. I stretched my legs and threw myself through the air.

It all went in slow motion. I saw the other side of the hole coming up toward me. I was going to make it! This wasn't so bad after all.

Then I saw I'd judged too quickly.

I tried to grab onto the other side of the hole and realized there was nothing to grab. The tips of my hands just brushed against where my feet should have landed. The kids gasped. I tried to hold on to something, anything, but it was no good.

Someone cried out as I fell. I could hear Dad's voice in my head, the same way it was always in my head when I did something wrong: *Stevie, you have to be careful about falling down tunnels.*

Whack! I hit the bottom of the hole. I was dazed and a little hurt, but it wasn't as bad as it could have been. Mostly I felt like an idiot. When I looked up, I could see the light of torches at the surface as kids bent their heads over the hole, trying to check on me.

"Stevie!" a kid called. "Are you all right? We can't see you!"

"I'm all right!" I called back. I didn't want to tell them I was hurt. I needed some milk and food to regain my health and feel better.

Then I stopped. I'd spoken too soon.

I wasn't alone down here.

CHAPTER 2

THE FIRST THINGS I SAW WERE THE EYES. PURPLE eyes that could never belong to a human. Then the creature in the darkness began to hiss.

It was an Enderman! And I'd just done the worst thing you can do if you see an Enderman. Normally these giant mobs were passive and left you alone, but if you looked at them in their eyes, they'd become hostile and attack.

The Enderman lunged toward me. All I had time to do was reach into my toolkit and pull out the first thing I found—a block of wood I'd gotten for myself earlier. I struck at the Enderman with the wood block, and it would have been a perfect hit, but the Enderman disappeared. A moment later I felt it right behind me, hissing in my ear.

I swung back at it with the wood block, yet the Enderman vanished just in time again. Along with being incredibly tall, Endermen also had the ability to teleport. So they were even harder to fight than your average mob.

I tried to shout to the kids above, telling them to throw my diamond sword down to me. Even if I could manage to hit the Enderman with the wood block, it wouldn't do much damage. I needed a real weapon! But when I attempted to call out, the Enderman popped right back up in my face, shrieking.

I dove down into a roll, trying desperately to pull some sort of a useful weapon from my toolkit. Somehow my hand reached in and pulled out my pick-axe. I jumped back to my feet and turned toward the Enderman, only to find it gone again. There was only a tiny bit of light from the opening above, and when the Enderman reappeared there a moment later, the light let me see the mob in all its terrifying detail. It was more than twice as tall as me, its long body the color of the darkness it had come out of.

Outside of that little bit of light from above, the tunnel was totally dark. I felt the Enderman pushing me back, deeper into the tunnel. Deeper into the complete blackness.

I had no idea how far the tunnel went. I might bump into a wall at any second and the Enderman would have me cornered.

Above me I could still hear kids yelling and screaming. They knew something was wrong, though they didn't know what. No one was jumping down to help me; I was on my own.

I swung back at the Enderman, making it disappear. As soon as it was gone, I tried running back toward the small area with light. When I took a step forward, I ran into something solid. A wall?

No, it was the Enderman, blocking my path to get out of there!

I'd never fought an Enderman before, let alone been all by myself against one in the dark. The Enderman reared over me and I ran deeper into the tunnel. Dad and people from the village liked mining, so there might be another exit in here somewhere. It was my only chance!

I hit a wall dripping with water. A dead end! The Enderman was almost on top of me, but then my hand reached to the side and felt nothing. That meant the tunnel turned to the right here! I bolted down that tunnel, my heavy breathing loud in my ears. All my senses were heightened and I expected to hit another wall any second. Panicked at this thought, I turned and swiped at the Enderman again, though of course all it did was teleport away and then appear right back in front of me.

I kept running, one hand holding my toolkit, another touching the tunnel's walls so I'd know if any more tunnels opened up.

As I turned a new corner I found myself face-to-face with the teleporting Enderman again. I swung out with all my might and this time managed to hit it. For a moment the Enderman flashed red, a signal that it had been struck.

The Enderman was taken aback for a second. This was what I needed. I struck again.

Another hit! Then the Enderman disappeared and I swung around in the darkness, looking for the return of purple eyes. Where was it?

I began running back to the direction of the hole to the cave . . . or what I thought was that direction.

Right then the Enderman showed up in front of me again, the purple of its eyes giving just enough light for me to see it barreling my way. I hit it as hard as I could and the Enderman let out a final shriek and it was gone. Gone for good.

However, there was no time to celebrate. I realized I was on unsteady ground, my feet half-standing on another hole. If I'd been less panicked and less hurt, I probably could have gotten my balance back. But I was exhausted. I fell down another hole in this forsaken tunnel, deeper into the darkness.

CHAPTER 3

"OOF!" I SAID WHEN I HIT THE GROUND. THANK-fully, this fall hadn't been as far as the first one, and this time I landed in an area with some light.

I was in a large, clear room underground, and ahead of me was an iron door with torches set around it. Still sore from my two falls, I got up and staggered toward the door, looking out in case any more Endermen or any other mobs showed up.

When I got closer to the door, I saw it had a symbol engraved on it. It kind of looked like the letters S and A, if you made them all fancy and combined them. It seemed familiar to me, although I couldn't think of why. I would have to ask Dad later.

Iron doors needed a switch to open, so I started searching the area. The switch was not far away and I snapped it. What was behind these doors? I was about to find out.

I was hoping it would be a stairway back to the surface, or maybe there was someone living underground there. As long as they could help me get out! However, when the door opened up to a new room, I was in for a surprise.

It was completely empty, except for one unopened treasure chest. My heart skipped a beat. A treasure chest would definitely turn this day around! I could go back up to the kids on the surface and tell them I had not only defeated the Enderman on my own, but I found a treasure chest full of goodies!

It's too bad my friends aren't here to see this, I thought as I approached the chest. I meant my *real* friends, not the village kids. Maison and Destiny and Yancy from Earth. And my cousin Alex, who lived in the next village over. Maison was the first person I met on Earth after I discovered a portal that led there. I met Destiny and Yancy a little later, and even though we weren't friends at first, we ended up becoming really close. I grew up with Alex, but we didn't become real friends until we fought Herobrine together. For all the recent adventures I'd been on, they'd been there to help me. Even that Enderman would have been a lot less scary if my friends had been here!

When I broke open the lid of the treasure chest, I leapt back and drew my weapon.

CHAPTER 4

THEN I HAD TO LAUGH AT MYSELF, EVEN THOUGH it wasn't funny. Boy, was I jumpy! There was something purple in the treasure chest, so the first thought my still-panicked brain had was that it was another Enderman. But Endermen all spawned at one height, and they were way too big to fit in treasure chests!

Slowly I reached inside and picked up the purple object. It felt warm on my palm and was glowing. It looked like . . . well, it looked kind of like an Ender crystal. Except it was too small to be one. Maybe it was a shard? But why would there be an Ender crystal shard here of all places?

I'd only seen Ender crystals once, and that was when I went to the End with my friends to fight Herobrine. We'd even seen the infamous Ender Dragon there, and we had seen her henchmen, the Endermen. Endermen sometimes came out to the Overworld, so it wasn't really shocking that I'd run into one. Just unusual. But the Ender Dragon and Ender crystal were *only* found in the End. No exceptions.

So this crystal had to be something else. I just couldn't think of what.

I picked the glowing purple crystal up, then turned and walked out of the room. It was like my own little torch, lighting my way with pale violet light. As I walked back, it made the tunnel seem less creepy and more magical.

I used my pickaxe to climb into the tunnel where I'd fought the Enderman and quickly made my way back. Because I was still feeling shaky, I kept my hand against the walls. I got mixed up a couple times, then found the dripping wall from before. That helped give me an idea of where I was. If a wall was dripping, I knew that meant there was water on the other end. It was amazing how the underground was its own little world.

Not a world I cared to visit again, though. Not for a long time.

There was light ahead! I started to jog, relieved I'd found the opening to the cave. As I got closer, I could hear all sorts of voices above talking very nervously.

"Something really bad happened to him down there!" I recognized the mocking boy's voice. "I told him not to try to jump over the hole, and then he did it anyway."

I remembered *again* why I wasn't good friends with the village kids.

I was going to shout that I was okay, but then another voice hissed, "*Find the shards!*"

I froze. "Hello?" I called out. There was no answer. Then I heard the voice again.

"*Find the shards and put them together! Only then will I be free!*"

It sounded like a woman's voice, except more menacing. The voice gave me the creeps, because on top of the scariness of it, I couldn't figure out where it was coming from. Was it an immediate threat? It didn't sound as if it were up in the cave with the others. It sounded so close, as if it were right next to me, and I knew that wasn't possible, because the crystal's light showed me I was alone in the tunnel. Then where could it be coming from?

CHAPTER 5

WHEN I HOISTED MYSELF BACK OUT OF THE hole and into the cave, I was surrounded by gawking kids who were all asking me what had happened. The mocking boy looked surprised to see me after all that. Dad was there and just getting ready to go down the tunnel after me.

"Stevie!" he said, in his Stevie-what-were-you-thinking? voice. It was a voice I knew like the back of my hand.

I started to hold up the purple crystal to show him, only to be interrupted. Dad wasn't done.

"I told you that if you wanted to see the other kids, you still had to stay in the village!" Dad went on. "You didn't even ask permission to be all the way out here! The blacksmith's gone missing, and I'm trying to help the village find him, then I get kids coming to me saying you're being attacked down below the surface!"

There was only one thing worse than falling down a hole, being attacked by an Enderman, and having kids mock you: when your dad yelled at you in front of all those kids afterward.

"But Dad—" I started to argue. Then I realized what he'd just said. "Wait, the blacksmith is missing?"

"He's not the only one," Dad huffed. "The mayor, the librarian, even the iron golems. Something is very wrong here, and I don't need to be chasing you down on top of it!"

"There was an Enderman—" I began. Dad cut me off.

"I'm sure there was!" he said. "If you'd stuck close to me, you'd know that in addition to so many villagers going missing, we've also had a number of Endermen harassing people around here. They're stealing blocks from people's houses and trying to get inside."

My head spun. Endermen were known for stealing blocks, and they'd hold the blocks at the very bottom of their long arms. However, everything else about this didn't seem right.

"Do you think the missing people and the Endermen are connected?" I asked.

"I don't know," Dad said. "And coming here to get you is wasting my time. Have some food, then grab your sword and let's go."

He pulled some food out of his toolkit, knowing I had to eat to regain my strength. It was a kind gesture, but he was looking so annoyed at me right then that it didn't feel very kind.

I couldn't even look at the kids, though I could feel their stares. Clutching the crystal close, I picked my diamond sword up and trotted after Dad, stuffing my face with the food he'd given me. I heard one of the kids say, "I told you that boy Stevie is strange. He's always messing things up and he only hangs out with weird-looking people from another world. Plus there's that crazy cousin of his, Alex. Does she ever *not* have her arrows?"

I wanted to turn back and say something, but I wouldn't let myself. If Dad heard it too, he didn't say anything.

The food was making my body feel better, though not my spirit. I really wanted to ask Dad what the crystal was and why I thought I heard a woman's voice down below. I wanted to ask him why I could make friends from other worlds, but not from my own.

However, I also didn't want to ask Dad anything right then. He had that concentrated look he always got when on a mission. I'd learned that when Dad was acting this way, you waited until he was done with his mission and then you asked questions. If you interrupted him, it'd just make him madder.

As we headed out of the cave, a man I didn't know came running over to us, shouting, "Steve! Stevie! Thank goodness I found you!"

The man was dressed like a guard and he was out of breath, as if he'd been looking for us for a while. I noticed he had said both of our names, Steve *and* Stevie. I was used to people searching for my dad when there were problems, not me.

"What is it, soldier?" Dad asked when the man got close.

"It's official business," the man said. "Mayor Alexandra needs to see both of you at once."

This caught my attention. Mayor Alexandra was Dad's sister and my aunt, and the mom of my cousin Alex. She was the mayor of the next village over, so this must've been one of her guards.

"Tell Alexandra it can wait," Dad said. "I need to help find the missing people in this village."

He tried to walk past the guard, but the guard stepped forcefully in front of him, blocking the way.

"It's an emergency," the guard said. "Mayor Alexandra is on her way here. Something is very wrong in our village. People are going missing, and we have Endermen breaking into people's homes and going through their things."

I gripped the crystal harder, as if it were some kind of protection against all this.

"The same thing is going on here," Dad said. "Has it reached other villages?"

"Not as far as I know," the guard said, shaking his head. "Just these two villages. It's as if the Endermen are . . . looking for something."

I felt as if I were in a daze. I slipped the purple crystal into my toolkit.

Before the guard could say anything else, we heard a horse's whinny. Aunt Alexandra's chariot came charging toward us, with my aunt clutching the reins. Next to her was my redheaded cousin Alex, and of course she was holding her bow and arrows. The kid I had heard earlier might have been making fun of her, but Alex *did* love her arrows, and she was the best shot around.

Aunt Alexandra vaulted out of the chariot before it even came to a full stop. I could see where Alex got her spitfire personality from. Aunt Alexandra and my dad were both famous in the area, and well-respected for their talents. People thought they'd make a perfect fighting team, but the truth was they didn't really like working together. A lot of times they'd just bicker as if they were still kids, fighting over who got the last piece of cake.

"We've been looking all over the village for you," Aunt Alexandra exclaimed as Alex got down beside her.

"I had to go look for Stevie," Dad said. "I was already trying to figure out what's going on with all the Endermen and the missing villagers. Do you have a plan for what to do next?"

"Yes," Aunt Alexandra said. I thought she would tell Dad what to do, so I was surprised when she turned her full attention on me.

"Stevie," she said, looking at me closely. "Go to Earth and get your friends. We have no time to spare."

CHAPTER 6

ARTH.

Earth was a world no one in the Overworld had known about before I accidentally discovered a portal to it. When I fell through the portal, I fell through my friend Maison's computer and into her house. Of course, she wasn't my friend yet, then. In fact, she thought I was some sort of monster and tried to fight me off with her baseball bat. It doesn't sound like the start of a good friendship, but it was.

On Earth, they had the Internet, cell phones, factories, fingers, and all sorts of crazy things you'd never see in the Overworld. The people look different too. Instead of being square like Overworld people, they tended to have emerald-shaped faces and proportioned bodies and hair that moves around and doesn't stick flat against their heads.

In the Overworld, everything and everyone has a squarish shape, and we all build our own things. We harvest our food, create our buildings from scratch, and live in a realm teeming with dangerous mobs. They don't have mobs on Earth, though they have their own dangers there. Sometimes they even turn things that are supposed to be helpful into something dangerous. Like that Internet thing they have. It lets them have all sorts of knowledge and information, but I'd seen them use their technology against one another before.

As different as our worlds are, there are lots of things we have in common too. We care about friends and family and taking good care of ourselves and eating good food. There are plenty of games we both like to play (even though I still don't really get baseball). And most of all, I know that whenever I need my Earth friends, they'll be there for me—even if they don't understand that a square world is much nicer to look at!—just as I knew they'd be there for me now.

Now, my special portal to Earth was kept in a secret room in my house, which only a very few people knew about. Because my Earth friends had helped in so many Overworld battles, some of the Overworld people learned about them, though they still didn't really understand where they came from. After getting Aunt Alexandra's command, Alex and I went running back to my home while the adults and the villagers all talked about what they had to do.

"Have you seen any of the Endermen?" Alex was asking me. "One came into my house while I was having my mushroom stew for lunch. It kept teleporting around the kitchen until I got it with my arrows! And look, it dropped an Ender pearl when I defeated it!"

Cheekily, Alex held up a glowing green Ender pearl. If you threw an Ender pearl, you'd teleport to where it landed. So it'd help you move fast, but it wasn't all good. Using an Ender pearl hurt your health, which was part of why I'd never used one myself. I'd always wanted to, and Dad said they came with a high cost and should only be used in emergencies.

I didn't want to tell Alex about my humiliating and scary fight with the Enderman earlier, so instead I pulled the purple crystal out of my toolkit. "Hey, have you ever seen something like this?" I asked. Alex liked to go exploring and she saw all kinds of stuff on her journeys.

Alex took the purple crystal and examined it. "It looks like an Ender crystal, except it's too small," she said. "Where did you find it?"

"In a tunnel below a cave," I said. I decided not to tell her how I got into that tunnel.

"Ooh, a new tunnel?" Alex said. "I'll have to check it out later. Maybe we can find some more of these."

Great. She'd probably drag me along with her too.

We came running up to my house and let ourselves in. Ossie, my cat, was there to greet us, but we didn't really have time to pet her. Together Alex and I opened the door to the portal room.

The portal was an amazing sight. It glowed green, blue and red, sort of reminding me of the Aurora Borealis pictures from Earth that Maison had shown me. As far as I knew, there was nothing else like it in the Overworld. The purple crystal seemed to glow brighter around it, or was that my imagination?

I was trying to figure out how I could tell Maison, Destiny, and Yancy we needed their help again. This wasn't their world, so wouldn't they get sick of coming here to battle all sorts of monsters they didn't have to deal with on Earth?

Then I noticed the inside of the portal was starting to shimmer like water that's been touched on the surface. Alex and I took steps back. Out of the portal jumped an Earth girl with black hair and brown skin, a baseball bat already in her hand.

"Maison!" I cried.

Maison came over and hugged me. A moment later two more people from Earth stepped out. There was Destiny, who was a little taller and rounder than Maison, with her brown hair and black clothes. Last of all there was Yancy, who was a teenager and a few years older than us. He was taller and paler than the rest of us, with slicked-back, black hair and a heavy jacket he wore even when it was warm out (he said it was "cool," whatever that meant). He'd also brought along his backpack, as if he were preparing to stay for a while.

"Why are you here?" I asked, amazed. "I was just going to go look for you! There are Endermen attacking the villages and people are missing."

"When I opened up *Minecraft* today, I knew something was off," Maison said. It was her game of *Minecraft* on her computer that allowed the Earth portal to even work. "So I called Yancy and Destiny over."

"Really?" I said. "I feel bad for asking you guys for help again . . ."

Destiny smiled shyly. She was usually pretty quiet, and she was great with computers. Yancy grinned at me and said, "Aww, Stevie, when life is nice and calm, it just doesn't feel normal. Where are the good ole days when I was turning into a zombie or getting blasted by a Wither?"

"Then you guys are really all here to help me?" I said. I thought of the kids earlier, who didn't even throw my diamond sword down to me when I needed aid.

"Of course," Maison said. "Now let's go get some Endermen!"

CHAPTER 7

WE WERE BACK AT THE VILLAGE, WITH Maison, Alex, Destiny, Yancy, and I all lined up in a row. Aunt Alexandra stood regally before us.

"You five have been called here for a very specific mission," Aunt Alexandra was saying.

Dad was standing to the side in disbelief. "Alexandra, they're kids—"

"They're kids who have saved both of us in the past, and all the worlds," Aunt Alexandra said. Turning back to us, she went on, "You're all aware of our current problems with Endermen and missing villagers. The adults are working on it, but we also want you here. I'm making your little group official. And I want to call you the Overworld Heroes."

"Overworld Heroes?" Yancy said, sounding shocked. Because of past not-so-good things he'd done, he wasn't used to people in the Overworld liking him.

Alex, on the other hand, gave a whoop. "Overworld Heroes!"

"You have saved us multiple times before," Aunt Alexandra said. "Each time you came together and defeated the enemy, despite the odds. I want you to be your own special task force, so that whenever we have issues in the Overworld, we are able to call on you."

My heart pounded.

"They have defeated enemies before, but is it really safe to put so much pressure on their shoulders?" Dad demanded.

Aunt Alexandra looked at him coolly. "I'm not saying we stand back and have them take care of everything. We'll be working against our enemies too, naturally. But whenever something is awry, I want to know we can call on you five. Are you kids all right with this? If you don't want to be in this task force, say so now, and I will not hold it against you."

Everyone but me cheered about being in the new task force, with Alex cheering the loudest.

"Stevie?" Aunt Alexandra said.

"Uh . . ." I looked at Dad, who was staring at me darkly. Probably thinking of how much I'd messed up earlier. How could I be on a special task force after how I bungled my fight against the Enderman? Maybe everything I'd done before was a fluke or luck. For someone who had managed to save the Overworld, I still messed up a lot.

My friends all looked at me. Aunt Alexandra's eyes were silently asking me to answer. So I said, "Okay." And I hoped I wouldn't regret it.

"I'm ready!" Yancy said, and reached into his backpack. He pulled out a Jack o' Lantern from the Overworld and plopped it on his head.

"Yancy!" Destiny hissed in a whisper. "It's probably disrespectful to wear that in front of a mayor!"

I don't know about disrespectful, though Yancy did look pretty funny with it on his head.

"This is me preparing for battle," Yancy said, with as much dignity as you can have with a pumpkin for a face. His voice was muffled. "Endermen don't attack you if you have a Jack o' Lantern on your head!"

I had forgotten all about this, but Yancy was right! He was already more prepared than I was, and he wasn't even from this world!

"Good thinking," Aunt Alexandra said. "Get to the bottom of this mystery as quickly as possible. Dismissed!"

CHAPTER 8

"OVERWORLD HEROES," ALEX SAID TO HERSELF, all moony-face and beaming. She kept tasting the words like really good cake. If any Endermen showed up, she'd probably be so lost in her own world she'd miss them. "Overworld Heroes."

"What is a hero, anyway?" I asked. We were all walking along the edge of the village, looking for clues. "Can you be born a hero?" I thought of my dad, because the village looked up to him so much.

"I think someone is a hero depending on their actions," Maison said. "Like if they singlehandedly defeat an army."

"I defeated an Enderman with my bow earlier!" Alex said proudly.

I grumbled something.

Yancy ran into a block in the middle of the street

and tripped. I had to catch him before he fell face first and smashed his Jack o' Lantern mask.

"Thanks, Stevie," Yancy said. He straightened the Jack o' Lantern. "These things never get easier to wear."

"You seem down," Destiny noted quietly, looking my way. Maison nodded, as if she'd noticed it too.

I looked at the five of us. We didn't seem like heroes. Heroes were supposed to be big and strong and not scared of anything.

"It's nothing," I said.

Yancy tripped over another block in the middle of the road.

"Ouch!" he said, getting back up. "Why are all these blocks in the road here?"

We got our answer immediately. An Enderman appeared down the road from us, holding a block in its long black arms. Its purple eyes locked on us and it began to advance.

Alex whipped out an arrow. Yancy, not able to see, asked, "What is it? What's going on?" The arrow went flying through the air—and the Enderman vanished, leaving an empty road.

"Did I get it?" Alex asked.

"Look out!" Maison cried. The Enderman had reappeared right behind Alex, leaning over her as if it wanted to whisper a secret. Or snatch her away in its clutches. Alex startled and tried to turn around in time. Maison flung her baseball bat out and the Enderman disappeared so that she couldn't touch it. But she'd saved Alex.

"An Enderman?" Yancy cried. He was trying to see it without taking off his Jack o' Lantern mask, but all he was doing was spinning around in confused circles and getting himself dizzy. The next moment a giant, night-black body was hovering over me like a shadow. It dropped the block it was holding. And it reached out to grab me.

CHAPTER 9

I SAW MAISON'S BASEBALL BAT SWINGING BEFORE THE mob could grab me, making the Enderman leave. It was scary to have something hulking over you like that, then have it be gone, then know it could show up *anywhere* in the next second. I was spinning around myself, trying to find it. The Enderman showed back up just next to Destiny, but instead of doing anything to her, it began moving quickly my way. Its purple eyes were on me and only me.

I threw out my sword when it got close. At the same time, Alex sent an arrow flying, Maison slammed her baseball bat into the Enderman, and Destiny struck it with a wooden sword she'd made. The Enderman was so into looking at me that the multiple strikes seemed to take it by surprise. It turned red for an instant, then disappeared before we could hit it again. The next moment it was on the roof of a nearby house, staring down at me with hostile eyes.

For a moment I thought of Alex's Ender pearl. If we threw it on the roof, we could teleport there. Then again, it would weaken our health, and by the time we got there, the Enderman would most likely be long gone.

Alex shot an arrow onto the roof and the Enderman easily dodged it by teleporting. I saw Alex's face go white in anger. She was a perfect shot and not used to her enemies being able to dodge so thoroughly.

"Stay still, you blasted Enderman!" she shouted.

"I can't take it anymore," Yancy said. "I need to see what's going on."

He pulled off his Jack o' Lantern. As soon as he did it, his eyes widened, because there was the Enderman in front of him, inches away.

Yancy had been so into the idea of his Jack o' Lantern keeping him safe that he didn't have any weapons at the ready. In a split second he yanked off his backpack and swung it out. The Enderman was there, then gone. It was back on the roof. It was behind us, making us all whirl around. It got behind us again, and we whirled again. And then it was right next to me, reaching for me again, its purple eyes towering over me, its whole body closing in around me like a black cloud.

CHAPTER 10

I SLASHED OUT WITH MY SWORD! AT THE SAME MO-
ment, Maison hit the Enderman with her baseball
bat, Alex struck it with an arrow, Destiny nailed it
with her wooden sword, and Yancy used his backpack.
It might have been a weird combination of weapons,
but it worked: the Enderman vanished for real this
time, dropping a green Ender pearl.

"Ooh, two Ender pearls in one day!" Alex gloated,
picking it up and tossing it in her hand. Ender pearls
were a rare find.

"It dropped something else," Maison said. "Huh . . .
what is that?"

It was another purple shard, like the one I'd found
earlier! What were the odds of that? Then I realized
something and dug my hand through my toolkit. No,
it wasn't another purple shard. It was the same one as

earlier, and it must have slipped out of my toolkit when I did my final lunge and slashed at the Enderman.

"That's mine," I said, a little embarrassed. "I found it earlier."

"That is awesome," Yancy said. "It's the color of an Ender crystal."

Maison reached down to pick it up. She examined it in her palm, then let out a cry and dropped it as if it had burned her.

"Maison, are you all right?" I exclaimed.

Maison didn't say anything at first. She was gripping her hand close and staring, wild-eyed, at the purple shard.

"Let me see your hand," Destiny said. When Maison opened her hand, it looked normal—no burns or anything. But Maison's eyes were still the same.

"It . . . it talked," Maison said.

"It talked?" we all repeated. None of us had heard anything. And there weren't any other people around this part of the village, so it's not like she could have overheard someone nearby.

"It was a woman's voice," Maison said, looking as if she were in a stunned trance. "Not like any voice I've heard, though. It was gravelly, and . . . I don't know . . . just really *scary*."

We all looked around. The area was totally empty.

"Let me see that," Yancy said. He picked up the purple shard hesitantly, as if he expected it to bite him.

Then, when nothing happened, he began tossing it back and forth in his hands the way I'd seen Maison do with a baseball. "It doesn't hurt to hold."

"No," Maison said. "The crystal doesn't hurt. The voice did. It felt *evil*."

We all looked around again.

"Maybe she heard an Enderman?" Destiny suggested.

"Endermen don't talk," Yancy said.

"Stranger things have happened, especially since the portal to Earth was first opened," Alex said dryly. In the past we'd had to fight a talking Wither, and that hadn't been normal, either.

"But we already defeated the Enderman," Destiny said. "How could it talk after it was gone?"

I was staring hard at Maison. "I heard that voice too," I said. "I was all alone in a tunnel and I heard it and there was no one around. What did it say to you?"

Maison took a long gulp. "It said, '*Get me out of this prison. I'm ready to rule again.*'"

CHAPTER 11

"**T**HE CRYSTAL!" DESTINY SAID. "MAYBE SOMEONE is trapped in the crystal!"

We all took turns looking deep inside the crystal and turning it this way and that. Nothing. I didn't think there was anything in the crystal, to be honest. I felt more like the crystal was connected to something.

I thought about what my friends and I had heard when we touched the crystal. *Find the shards and put them together! Only then will I be free! Get me out of this prison. I'm ready to rule again.*

"Do you think the crystal talked?" Yancy said.

"Crystals can't talk," Alex said. "Besides, how come none of us can hear it?" She took the crystal from Yancy and held it, then put it up to her ear like a seashell from Earth. "I don't hear a thing."

Maison was rubbing her arms as if she were very, very cold.

"I know I heard something!" she said. "It was like the voice was in my mind!"

I stood up straighter and nodded. That was the perfect way of saying it! It had been this very threatening, malicious voice . . . and it had been in my head without me thinking it. Somehow the crystal was letting us hear someone who wasn't there!

I got all excited that I had figured it out, then I realized how crazy that sounded. That couldn't be right, could it?

"Let's go talk to my dad and Aunt Alexandra," I said. "Maybe they know something about this."

Yancy tossed the purple crystal up in the air and caught it. "Okay," he said. "But where did you find this exactly, Stevie? Spill the beans."

"What?" I said, confused. "I don't have any beans." That was some kind of food they had on Earth, and it's not like this was a good time to eat with so much danger around.

"He means tell him everything," Destiny said.

Uh-oh. That was the last thing I wanted to do. Yancy handed me the purple crystal back and looked at me expectantly.

I would have given anything for a distraction. Unfortunately, I got the worst kind of one. I blinked, and then there were three Endermen circling us.

CHAPTER 12

THEY WEREN'T JUST COMING IN CLOSER FOR THEIR prey—they were coming in closer for me! Their purple eyes saw only me. Their arms were lifted to grab only me.

I struck out with my sword when they got right up next to me. They vanished, but I knew better than to think they'd been defeated. Then, like the Enderman in the tunnel earlier, all three of them were directly behind me, breathing down my neck.

As I rolled into a dodge, the others all rushed toward the Endermen. It was like a bad game, because all the Endermen did was disappear and show up again. How could you defeat a whole group of them when they had skills like that? Did we all have to make ourselves Jack o' Lanterns or something? That would take some time, and the Endermen might get us in the meanwhile!

"Stop them!" Alex said. "They want Stevie."

"No!" Maison said. "They want the crystal!"

The crystal? I tucked it back into my toolkit and rose back up with my sword.

"Whatever they want, we have to stop them!" Yancy was hitting at them with his backpack and trying to put his Jack o' Lantern back on at the same time. He couldn't do both, so he was stuck defending himself. The Endermen began swirling around us like a tornado, here one second, gone the next, reappearing with outstretched arms.

One Enderman was shorter than the others, like the size of an Overworld man. That didn't make it much less threatening, though. It seemed like the most aggressive one, getting inches from me again and again. It opened its mouth in a terrible hiss right in front of my face, its angry purple eyes bearing down on me. I attempted to hit it with my sword. No luck! It was gone and then back again, right by my side.

Then a fourth Enderman showed up on top of one of the houses. It stood there a moment as if it were watching the scene. Then its eyes landed on me and a strange, fierce hunger came over its expression.

"There's another one!" I shouted. It wasn't a moment too soon. The Enderman teleported from the roof and down into the street in front of us, knocking right into Alex, who was facing the other way. Alex cried out and dropped her arrows.

"Alex!" I ran over to her. I wanted to help, but I ended up running right into the thick of things. There was still the Enderman right next to her, and as soon as I was at Alex's side, the other three surrounded me like a fence, trapping me in the middle and keeping everyone else out.

"Stevie!" I heard the others call. Between the huge bodies of the Endermen I saw Maison frantically swinging her baseball bat and Alex shooting her arrows. They hit the Endermen, but the Endermen didn't even flinch when they turned red. Four pairs of long black arms reached toward me. One of them grabbed me by the middle and began to carry me away, knocking the diamond sword out of my hand.

CHAPTER 13

THE ENDERMAN'S ARMS WERE OVER MY STOMACH like a vice. Instead of carrying a block, like Endermen are known to do, it was carrying me! It turned in the direction that led out of the village, and then it teleported with me.

For a moment there was nothing. The whole world blurred until all I saw was a variety of colors, smashed together like a painting. Blurry green for the grass mixed with shady brown from the trees. Some silver gray for clouds thrown in. It didn't feel as if there was any air.

Then everything came back to normal. I realized the Enderman had teleported us straight out of the village to the fields nearby. When I looked behind us, I could see Maison and the others, but they were all small in the distance like dolls. They were shouting and running toward me.

The Enderman seemed to sense this, because then it teleported again. The world went blurry and I couldn't breathe. Then it was like being underwater and looking at the surface, with all the colors moving and shimmering and making no real sense. A moment later we returned to reality and I saw we were even farther from the village. My friends were still all running toward me as fast as they could, and they looked even farther away than before!

I tried to struggle out of the Enderman's grip, but it was too strong! I'd lost my sword, though I still had my toolkit on me. Something in there would have to protect me, or I was done for!

My hand went into the toolkit and closed around something I'd momentarily forgotten. The crystal! I yanked it out so I could see it, watching as it glowed especially bright, as if it had a little sun in it.

The Enderman teleported again. When I lost my chance to breathe for a third time, I realized I didn't have a choice here. I had to do something! As soon as we teleported back into existence, I took a huge gasp of air to fill my lungs. And then I hit one of the Enderman's arms with the crystal, using all my strength.

There was an explosion of purple light. I fell out of the Enderman's hands and rolled to the ground. The Enderman let out a noise that sounded almost human. I heard the heavy sound of it collapsing to the ground behind me.

Shaken, gasping for breath, I rolled over to see what had happened. My eyes widened. At first I didn't understand what I was seeing.

Someone was kneeling in the exact same spot the Enderman had been, touching his face as though he couldn't believe it.

"No way," I whispered.

"Stevie," the man moaned. "Thank you, thank you. Can you ever forgive me?"

It was the missing blacksmith!

CHAPTER 14

"WHERE DID THE ENDERMAN GO?" I EX-claimed.

"Don't you understand?" the black-smith said. "I *was* the Enderman!"

Maison and the others all came racing up to us, completely out of breath.

"He—he changed!" Alex wheezed. "There was an—Enderman—then a light—then a man!"

"When I opened my shop this morning, there were two Endermen there, going through my things," the blacksmith said. "They closed in on me, and they turned me into . . . into . . ."

"They turned you into an Enderman?" I said. "Wait, does that mean . . .?"

"The missing villagers!" Maison said, getting it.

The blacksmith nodded grimly. "Yes," he said.

"All of the missing villagers have been turned into Endermen too. It's like how zombies can create zombie villagers."

"So Endermen can create villager Endermen?" Yancy said. "I've never heard of that, and I'm a big *Minecraft* buff."

"*Minecraft*?" the blacksmith repeated, confused.

"On Earth, they call our world *Minecraft*," I explained to him.

The blacksmith shook his head. "There is some dark magic going on. What's happening now isn't normal. When I turned into an Enderman, it clouded my thoughts. I just knew I had to attack, and I had to find . . . to find . . ." He seemed to be having a hard time getting the words out.

"To find what?" I asked.

"That crystal!" he said, pointing toward it. "There was a voice in my head that kept telling me to find that crystal and bring it back to her, no matter what."

"*Her?*" I repeated.

Maison had the same chilled look she had earlier when she touched the crystal. "I think Stevie and I heard the same voice when we touched the crystal," she said. "Did it sound very angry and evil?"

"Yes!" the blacksmith said. "That's a good way to describe it, but once I was an Enderman, there was no way I could resist that voice. I had to obey it. There was still a part of me—the real me—left, but it got to be less and less as time went on. I'm convinced that if you hadn't changed me back, I would have turned fully into an Enderman. Forever." He shivered and looked haunted by his own thoughts.

"Do you have any idea whose voice it is?" I demanded. I was feeling haunted too. What would that be like, to become an Enderman and lose yourself? It was scary enough being in the clutches of an Enderman!

"No," the blacksmith said. "But she is very old and very powerful. She has been in hiding for thousands of years, and she needs the crystal to get back. The Endermen are her servants and she's using them to make more servants by making more Endermen."

"We have to tell my mom and Uncle Steve about this," Alex said. "Can the crystal be used to turn other villagers human again?"

With shaky hands the blacksmith reached out as if he wanted to hold the crystal. I gave it to him. He marveled at it in his hand.

"There is definitely magic in this crystal," he said. "Some sort of very ancient, very strong enchantment."

Enchantment? I knew in the Overworld you could enchant different objects, but that was way beyond anything I could do. Even Dad didn't go much for enchantments.

"Maybe the Endermen want it because they don't want us to be able to turn the villagers back," Destiny said.

"I think that's part of it, but I think it goes much deeper than that." The blacksmith handed the crystal back to me and massaged his temples. "I'm forgetting what I knew and felt as an Enderman. It's fading like a dream and I feel more human. I'm scared I'm forgetting information that would be helpful to you."

"Tell us everything you remember," Maison said comfortingly, putting a hand on his shoulder. "And we'll head back into the village to tell everyone your story and what we know now."

"And guard that crystal," Yancy said, eyeing it.

I nodded and swallowed. We turned toward the direction of the village—but's that's when we realized there would be no easy passage for us. The other three Endermen we fought earlier were coming toward us, ready to continue the battle.

CHAPTER 15

"**A**RE THEY VILLAGERS TOO?" I ASKED. I HAD A sudden, terrible thought. What if the Endermen I'd defeated earlier had been villagers? It was too late to change them back now!

"No," the blacksmith said. He rose to his feet and stared the Endermen down. "The ones who were human are still as tall as humans. These are all real Endermen."

That was a relief. However, that also meant we had a lot of villagers to save, and we needed to get into the village as fast as possible to tell the others. Even if I hadn't defeated any villager-Endermen, what if someone else had?

"Where's my sword?" I cried, remembering I didn't have it. And the others weren't holding it, so it must still be back in the village.

"We left it!" Alex said. "Saving you was more important!"

I understood why they had ignored the sword and come after me. It didn't do me much good now, though! That diamond sword was my best weapon. Then the blacksmith said, "Use the crystal, Stevie. It has more than one use."

An Enderman teleported so that it was right in front of me, and I struck it with the crystal. It was a direct hit, but the Enderman still disappeared and showed up safely a few blocks away.

"It didn't do anything!" I said.

"Try again!" the blacksmith said.

What if he was wrong? If the crystal didn't work, we might lose any chance we had of fighting back.

The second of the three Endermen zeroed in on me and I hit it with the crystal. Same result. It got hit and then reappeared a moment later, just fine. Even with a special crystal, fighting Endermen was so aggravating!

The first Enderman was back in front of me. I brought back my arm and hit it with the crystal as hard as I could. The Enderman turned bright red and was gone for good.

"Two hits!" I cried. "One hit to change a villager back, two hits to defeat an Enderman!" This was much better than all the times you had to hit an Enderman with a sword to defeat it.

There were two Endermen remaining now. The one that had already come at me was approaching again, and when I hit it with the crystal, it was gone.

"This is going to make things so much easier!" I said, feeling real relief for the first time that day.

The third Enderman was watching us from the shade of a nearby oak tree, its eyes like glowing purple fire. Its stare was so intense that I started to sweat.

Then the Enderman was next to Yancy, snatching his backpack.

"Hey!" Yancy said. "Bring that back!"

The Enderman ignored him. It teleported farther out into the fields, its two long arms in front of its body, holding the backpack like a block.

"Bring that back!" Yancy said, starting to run toward it.

"Don't!" Alex said. "Let it leave! It's not like that backpack was a good weapon, anyway."

The Enderman disappeared and reappeared even farther out. It still had the backpack. Then it disappeared again and reappeared as a black dot in the distance.

"What did it want my backpack for?" Yancy grumbled. "My homework is in there!"

"Feel lucky it's leaving us alone," Alex said, looking at Yancy skeptically.

"But this means I have to redo my homework," Yancy said, as if this were the worst thing in the world.

"It's not like I can tell my teachers that an Enderman stole my homework."

"Tell them your dog ate it," Alex said.

"Yeah, they don't believe that one, either," Yancy said.

The Enderman was completely out of sight by now. I should have been relieved, but instead I felt a new worry. Why was the Enderman so interested in Yancy's backpack? It didn't have the crystal. *I* did. And why would an Enderman leave after attacking someone? Did it see what I'd done to the other Endermen and decide to save itself? I didn't think Endermen used that kind of logic. When they were hostile, mobs only had one thought: *attack, attack, attack.*

"Let's get to the village before anything else weird happens," I said, eyeing the horizon.

CHAPTER 16

WHEN WE SKIDDED INTO THE VILLAGE, I SAW some armored guards going from building to building, their weapons at the ready. They must be checking each building for Endermen. Other than that, the village looked like a ghost town. And it was eerily quiet.

"Where is everyone?" I asked, holding my diamond sword. I felt a lot more confident now that I'd picked it back up. But where were all the villagers? Had they all been turned into Endermen?

Fortunately not. As we ran into the village, I could see people's faces through windows. They were in hiding. Whole families were huddled together, looking out the windows with scared, worried eyes.

"The village must be on lockdown until they figure out what's going on," Alex said.

We came up to the armored guards.

"What are you kids doing out here?" one of them demanded. "You should be home with your parents!"

"We're the Overworld Heroes," Alex said proudly, puffing out her chest. "Our parents *told* us to be out here."

The armored guards looked at her skeptically. Then they looked over our whole group more closely. They were surprised to see the Earth people, but their real shock was when they saw the blacksmith with us, safe and sound.

"There you are!" one guard said. "Where have you been?"

"No time for details," the blacksmith said. "We need to find Steve and Mayor Alexandra so they can form a plan against the Endermen."

"They're in the building at the end of the street," a guard said, pointing.

That was all we needed to hear. The six of us tore down the rest of the street until we reached the final building. It had an iron door and I pounded on it, calling, "Dad! Dad! Open up!"

The door immediately flew open. Dad looked so relieved. "I was just going to look for you!" he said. "We had a kid go missing while you were gone. No one is safe here."

"But Dad!" I said. "We figured it out! Look!"

I held up the purple crystal. "It has some kind of

special magic," I said. "I found it in the tunnel earlier. The Endermen all want it and they know it's around here somewhere. And there's a voice, a really evil-sounding voice!"

"What?" Dad said. "A voice? Slow down, Stevie."

I was standing in the doorway, out of breath. The others were all trying to crowd around me and there wasn't enough room for everyone to stand in the doorway. Aunt Alexandra came over, holding a map of the area and a scroll that had a list of people's names. The blacksmith's name was on it, so I realized she was keeping track of all the people who'd gone missing in this village and in hers. The map also had markings of where the people had been last seen.

"I heard the voice when I picked up the crystal, and so did Maison!" I hurried on. "The voice said she's in a prison. And she needs this crystal to get free!"

"That doesn't make any sense, Stevie," Dad said. "Crystals don't work as keys. This doesn't look like anything."

He took it from me and held it. I was hoping he'd hear the voice too so he'd understand what was going on. Nothing seemed to be happening.

"The boy's right, Steve," said a voice behind us. We all made room so the blacksmith could walk into the building.

Dad's and Aunt Alexandra's eyes widened.

"Blacksmith!" Dad said. "Where have you been? Do you know where the others are?"

"They're all in this area, looking for that crystal," the blacksmith said. "You see—"

He didn't get a chance to finish his sentence. Behind us we heard another sound, and this time it was a terrible hissing. It was that awful sound Endermen make when they're about to attack.

We all whirled around. There was an Enderman, and it wasn't any taller than me! It still looked vicious, though, with its mouth opened like an animal showing its fangs and its purple eyes sharp as ice.

I remembered what the blacksmith had said earlier. If this Enderman was my height, did that mean it was a kid from the village? The one who was missing?

Dad had already grabbed his sword and was raising it over the Enderman to finish it off. "Be gone, Enderman!" he shouted.

"Dad, no!" I cried.

CHAPTER 17

MY SHOUT DISTRACTED DAD FOR AN INSTANT. That was enough for the little Enderman to teleport farther away from the building and to safety.

"Stevie, what were you thinking?" Dad exclaimed, frustrated.

I didn't get a chance to answer, because the next second the little Enderman was back and standing in the building with us. Dad swung his sword and the Enderman disappeared and reappeared, right next to me this time.

"Hit it with the crystal!" I yelled to Dad.

Dad must have thought I was acting crazy, because he ignored me. He tried to hit the Enderman with his sword again. When the Enderman disappeared safely, I ran forward to Dad and snatched the crystal back.

"Stevie, not now!" Dad said. "Listen to me!"

I wanted to tell *him* to listen. But the best thing to do was just show him. I spun around, looking in every corner of the room, trying to figure out where the little Enderman had gone. And then I felt it right behind me.

Fast as a flash, I whirled around and struck its shoulder with the crystal. This time I was able to see what happened. First there was an explosion of purple light. It made the whole room turn violet for a few seconds and people were shielding their eyes with their hands.

Inside the light I saw the shape of the Enderman change. The long arms and legs returned to a normal length. Then the light was gone and there was an Overworld boy there, looking shaken and relieved.

I couldn't believe my eyes. It was the boy who had been mocking me so much earlier!

"It's the missing boy!" Aunt Alexandra said, her hand to her mouth.

Dad wasn't even able to talk at first. He'd been *this* close to getting the kid with his sword because he'd looked like an Enderman.

Then Dad slowly turned his eyes my way. Even though he still wasn't saying anything, I could see he wanted to thank me. His eyes held an apology—they were the exact opposite of the eyes that were so frustrated at me earlier today.

"The Endermen are turning villagers into Endermen," the blacksmith said. "The villagers look exactly like Endermen except for their size."

As the blacksmith was explaining to Dad how his brain had been clouded and he'd been trying to find the crystal, I squatted down next to the mocking boy. I guessed I shouldn't think of him as the "mocking boy" anymore, though. Now he was looking at me like he was glad I was there—and like he expected me to hate him for what he'd done.

So I just asked him, "What happened?"

"My parents told me to stay inside, but I wanted to see the Endermen," he said. "I wanted to be a hero. I wanted glory. So I went outside and . . ." He gulped. "An Enderman grabbed me. And the next thing I knew, there was this evil voice, telling me to get the crystal . . ."

I noticed Dad and the blacksmith had both stopped talking and were watching the boy. The blacksmith was nodding along, because he'd had the same experience. Dad looked shocked, as if he still didn't believe it. I didn't think he *wanted* to believe it.

"We need to get him home to his parents," Aunt Alexandra said, taking charge. "Ask the librarian if they've ever heard of a crystal like this. Maybe we can figure out why the Endermen want it so badly."

"The librarian is one of the missing people," Dad reminded her.

Aunt Alexandra's face clouded. "Right. But once we find the librarian . . ."

"If you hit an Enderman villager with the crystal once, they turn back," I said. "If it's a real Enderman, you can defeat them in two hits with the crystal."

"But what is this evil voice you were talking about?" Dad asked.

The blacksmith, the boy, Maison, and I all shuddered, because we'd heard it. Everyone else was just looking at us, trying to figure out how a voice could be so bad.

"I'll take the boy home," the blacksmith offered. "He lives close to my smithy. In the meantime . . ."

"In the meantime," Aunt Alexandra said, holding up her scroll, "we have to get all these villagers turned human again. Before they're changed forever."

CHAPTER 18

WHILE THE BLACKSMITH TOOK THE BOY home, the rest of us went out into the empty streets of the village, hunting for villager-Endermen we could turn back. We had to be wary because of the tricky way Endermen moved around. Even if an Enderman happened to be a villager on the inside, that didn't mean it wouldn't attack us while it was an Enderman. We had to defend ourselves while trying to protect the villager-Endermen, which made it extra difficult.

As we turned on the second street, an Enderman popped in front of us. It was Dad's height, so I knew it was a villager.

"Now, Stevie!" Dad said, trying to keep the Enderman at bay. I rushed up and hit it with the crystal. There was the same flash of light, and then there

62

was the missing mayor from this village. He fell to the ground, gripping his head.

"That voice, that voice!" he said. "You made that voice go away!"

Dad glanced at me. He seemed to be realizing just how terrifying that voice was.

"I'm the mayor the next village over," Aunt Alexandra said. "So I took charge in your absence." She told him what was going on as she checked off his name on the list. You had to give it to Aunt Alexandra: after so many years in public service, she knew how to keep her cool and keep working in the strangest situations.

"I think we should have everyone come out of their houses and meet in the center of the village," Aunt Alexandra said. "That way we can better keep track of people, and we can watch for more Endermen."

The mayor ran off to get started on this.

We wandered the village. It was much easier changing people back with Dad there, because he had more experience in battle. Alex was there to help him with her arrows. People began to come out to the center of the village, sticking close together. I saw the mocking boy and his mom were there too. The people were watching us as we made our way through the village, their desperate eyes asking us to make things right again.

Is that what it means to be a hero? I thought. I was mulling over what the mocking boy had said earlier.

He'd gone out to "be a hero" but he wasn't prepared, and all he'd done was get himself captured. Instead of helping the fight, he'd made it more difficult because he'd become one of the enemies. Is that what happened when you rushed into things?

There were plenty of times *I'd* rushed into things too. Was it just sheer luck I'd been okay so far? Sometimes I thought it was that. I had to make up plans right in the moment because something unexpected happened. In the Overworld, you had to be ready for anything in order to survive. And I guessed that included magical purple crystals and special Endermen.

As we turned people back, we kept asking them what they knew. They all had the same stories: they were captured. There was a hideous voice telling them what to do and they had to obey it. The voice was demanding her freedom, but something about the way she talked told all of us that there was a *reason* she was locked up somewhere.

"There's another one!" Maison called, bringing me out of my thoughts. An Enderman was coming out at us from between two nearby houses. It was about Dad's height, so we knew it was a villager. That meant we had to wait for it to come toward us until it got close enough that I could get it. Dad and the others were crowded close around in case the Enderman tried to hurt me while it went after the crystal.

That didn't mean it wasn't nerve-wracking to

stand there and watch Enderman after Enderman come at me, hissing and vicious, arms out to grab. I had to trust that Dad and the others would make sure another Enderman didn't snatch me up and teleport away again.

The villager-Enderman bolted for me but I was too quick. It felt the purple crystal strike its shoulder before I felt its long arms on me. Another flash of light. Another person saved.

Aunt Alexandra was checking the names off on her list. Everyone who we'd turned back already had their name on there.

"That's good," Aunt Alexandra was murmuring to herself as she looked over the list. "There are only two names left."

As if it sensed we'd been talking about it, another villager-Enderman showed up nearby. It was walking forward, then twisted its head to peer our way. Its eyes showed a jolt of recognition when it saw the crystal.

"Get ready, Stevie," Dad said, holding his sword tight.

I took a deep breath and nodded.

The Enderman came quickly at me, and I went to strike it with the crystal. But it vanished. It appeared next to Maison, who tried to push it over my way with her baseball bat. The Enderman looked at her strangely. That was good enough for me; it gave me a chance to lunge at it with the crystal. A moment later a woman was in the Enderman's place, crumpled on the ground, stunned but safe.

"Fantastic!" Aunt Alexandra said, making a note. "That means there's only one person left."

"Don't you think there's something fishy about all this?" Alex asked.

"What do you mean?" Aunt Alexandra looked up from her list.

"Before there were real Endermen going around our villages," Alex said. "We've walked the whole village now, and the only Endermen we've run into have been villagers. Where did all the real Endermen go? Why would they suddenly abandon their mission?"

Aunt Alexandra started to say something, but I couldn't hear her. My eyes were on the horizon. The whole line of it was turning black along the edge. And it was moving.

I didn't have any words to say. All I could do was point.

Everyone looked at the horizon.

As the black line got closer, it became clearer. It wasn't a single line. It was a mass of Endermen. *Real*, gigantic Endermen, their arms outstretched, coming our way.

Coming for me. Coming for the crystal.

CHAPTER 19

"**T**HERE'S NO WAY . . ." AUNT ALEXANDRA BEGAN. She wasn't able to look away from the approaching army of Endermen. "We don't have enough villagers here to stand a chance."

"We can get fighters from other villages," Dad said.

"There's not enough time, and you know it!" Aunt Alexandra snapped. "We have to evacuate. It's our only chance."

"We can't let the Endermen take over the village!" Dad protested. "What if they destroy everything?"

"I don't hear you coming up with anything better, Steve!"

Evacuate? That meant running and leaving everything behind. It might save us for the time being, sure. But as long as I had this crystal shard, I knew the Endermen would keep following me.

"I can't believe it," Yancy said, shaking his head. At first I thought he was talking about the sheer number of Endermen heading our way. Then I saw something else had caught his attention. One Enderman was walking ahead of the rest, as if it were a general leading them our way. And it was holding Yancy's backpack. It must have been the Enderman from before, the one that had fled!

"It's like it told them where they could find the crystal," I said, stunned. "So they all regrouped for one massive attack." I gripped the crystal even tighter, knowing that I had to protect it, no matter what.

"Maybe we can hide the crystal on Earth," Destiny suggested.

"But what if they find the portal and attack Earth?" Maison said.

I could see the center of the village from where we were standing, and the other villagers had all crowded there. They were panicking, so they must not have known what to do, either. Dad and Aunt Alexandra were still bickering, because both of them were convinced they had the best idea of what to do, and they weren't going to listen to the other. All I could see was that they were wasting time!

Finally we could see the horizon line after the mass of black. I looked over the Endermen that were coming at us, and there had to be hundreds of them.

"You don't know what you're doing, Alexandra!"

Dad ranted. "We run some people to the next village and get supplies, and then . . ."

"And then those of us who stay are turned into Endermen!" Aunt Alexandra shot back. "We have to evacuate together."

"That's a cowardly thing to do," Dad said.

"It's not cowardly if it saves people! Even you know that sometimes you have to pull back. It's not the same as surrendering! This is war, and we need a strategy."

"Strategy!" Dad said. "Your strategy is to put a group of kids in charge of saving the Overworld!"

For the first time they seemed to remember that we were there. Both of them looked our way.

The pressure was on us. Aunt Alexandra looked at us as if she were silently begging for a great idea. Dad looked like he thought we were in over our heads.

Maison was the first to talk. "I don't think we can defeat the Endermen in one-on-one fights because of how many there are," she said. "We have to do something to take them all out at once."

"Like TNT," Yancy cut in. "Do you have any TNT?"

"Yes," Dad said. "But that will destroy the village too."

"Besides," Alex said, "they might just teleport around the TNT to come after us."

"Well, what destroys Endermen?" Yancy said. He started counting ideas off on his fingers. "Lava does.

That'd be hard to find around here, though. There's water. Can we get the Endermen to follow us toward some nearby lake or something?"

"There is a lake nearby," Dad said. "However, I still don't know that it will work. You would have to get the Endermen to follow you into the water, and not teleport in front of you while you're heading there."

"It's the best we have," Aunt Alexandra said.

"Stevie?" Maison said, waving her hand in front of my face. "Are you still there?"

I came out of my thoughts. As soon as Yancy had mentioned water, my mind had wandered to this morning. That dark tunnel. The twists and turns. The dripping water . . .

"There's water down below, in the tunnel," I said. "If we get the Endermen to follow us down there, we can knock out the blocks and flood the place." It would be very dangerous, but I didn't want to admit that. Because I knew the alternative was to try to fight the army coming toward us. "I think it's the best chance we have."

CHAPTER 20

"**N**O, STEVIE," DAD SAID. "YOU COULD DROWN!
We'll go to the lake instead."

"Stevie's right," Yancy said. "If it's underground, they won't be able to escape so easily, and the
rushing water will catch them by surprise. I don't think
we have any better ideas. And people are better swim-
mers than mobs, so I don't think it's as dangerous as
you believe."

Dad mulled this over. Saying you didn't think it
was *as* dangerous didn't mean it wasn't incredibly
dangerous.

"Stevie and I can go together," Yancy said, slinging
a friendly arm over my shoulder. "I'll put my Jack o'
Lantern back on, and that will throw the Endermen
off a little."

"Destiny and I can help fight off Endermen,"

Maison said, clutching her baseball bat. "And we'll follow you to the tunnel so we can back you up if there are any problems."

I nodded. Part of me was looking at Maison, and another part was looking at the Endermen. They'd almost reached the village now.

"Give me this chance, Dad," I said, looking up at him. Right then he looked so tall and distant he might as well have been an Enderman. I knew he was only trying to protect me because I was his kid, but he might be sacrificing the whole village to do it. I knew then that even though Dad could get really frustrated with me, he cared about me more than anything else.

"I know I messed up earlier," I went on. "But I was also right about the Endermen. I think we can do this as a team, like we've done other things with teamwork."

Dad looked at me for a moment. "You've amazed us before, Stevie," he said. "Go amaze us again." Then he ran into the village, yelling for everyone's attention. Many people were running into their houses or fleeing the village instead of fighting.

For a moment I let those words sink in, my heart pounding.

"Which way to the tunnel?" Yancy asked, putting the Jack o' Lantern back on his head and adjusting it.

"That way," I said, pointing.

"What way?" Yancy said, not seeing.

Maybe this wasn't such a good plan after all. "To your right," I said. "Yancy, I don't know about this. We want the Endermen to chase us, so there's really no point in the Jack o' Lantern."

"We want the Endermen to chase *you*," Yancy corrected as if I were being silly. "If they're not aware of me being there, I can help you fight them off."

I still didn't agree, because the Endermen were basically ignoring everyone other than me, anyway. Yancy was making this more complicated than it had to be.

"All right, fine," Yancy said, pulling off the Jack o' Lantern. And then he walked directly into an Enderman.

CHAPTER 21

THE ENDERMAN HISSED. IT WAS THE ONE WITH Yancy's backpack, and it threw the backpack to the side and thrust its arms out at Yancy, trying to grab him. It would have gotten him too, if an arrow hadn't come flying out of nowhere and struck the Enderman. In a split second Alex had pulled out her bow and saved Yancy. The Enderman startled, and a second later Maison and Destiny jumped on it with their weapons, finishing it off.

The next moment several more Endermen appeared around us, circling us, closing us in. I tried to look for Dad, to see if he'd come back and help us, but he'd disappeared somewhere in the village. We were all alone out here.

"Stop them!" Aunt Alexandra said, raising her diamond sword.

We had even less time than I realized! Endermen were rapidly making their way through the village, teleporting several blocks at a time. Almost as soon as they reached the village, they reached us. In less than a minute we would probably have the whole army of hundreds all around us, and the villagers wouldn't be able to fight them off and free us. The tunnel idea wasn't going to work, though it wasn't because of the danger—we didn't have a way to make it there in the first place!

We were all fighting as best as we could, but it had turned to in-the-moment self-defense when we should have been running ahead. Looming, night-black bodies with purple eyes kept flashing in front of me, being knocked back by my sword or someone else's weapon, but always reappearing.

"There's no way to fight them when they're teleporting!" I exclaimed.

As soon as I said it, I realized what I was saying.

There was only one way to get on even footing with a mob that can teleport. You have to be able to teleport yourself.

Like going down into the tunnel and flooding it with water, this was going to come with great risks. Then again, what choice did we have?

"Alex!" I cried above all the noise. "We need your Ender pearls!"

CHAPTER 22

HERE WAS ALEX? THE ENDERMEN WERE pressing in closer and closer. I lost sight of all my friends, because there was just the crush of Enderman bodies, coming in to seize the crystal. If I took a step back, I'd run into an Enderman. If I took a step forward, one would snatch me. They were at all sides of me, so it was like being in a rapidly moving storm cloud.

An arrow hit the Enderman directly in front of me and it vanished. There was Alex, struggling to get through. The Endermen were pushing all against us. I reached for Alex's hand and was pressed back. I reached again, and this time I was able to take both Ender pearls from her.

I threw the first Ender pearl up into the air so that it would go over the Endermen's heads. I couldn't see where it was going to land, and I hoped I threw it far enough away from the attacking mobs.

I knew the second the Ender pearl hit the ground. Everything went blurry again and my breath got sucked out of me. I tried to pull more air in, and it felt as if there were nothing there! The colors kept swirling like paint.

Then I landed on the other side of the Endermen, on my stomach, as if I'd fallen. The pain felt like a mob had attacked me and I'd taken a direct hit to the gut. I tried to get back up on shaky feet. What I really needed was food and milk to feel better, and I knew I wasn't going to be getting those things for a while. I had to ignore the pain and keep going.

But as soon as I rose, something grabbed me from behind and lifted me into its clutches.

CHAPTER 23

THOUGHT I WAS DONE FOR. BUT IT WAS YANCY! THE Jack o' Lantern was long gone and he looked ready for action.

"This way, right?" Yancy said, running toward the cave.

It took me a winded second to understand what he was talking about. "Yeah!" I said. "It's inside a cave. You'll never miss it!"

The Endermen, meanwhile, had realized the crystal shard and I weren't where we'd been. They'd stopped attacking Aunt Alexandra and my friends and were looking around. It didn't take long for them to figure out where I was. They began to teleport, chasing after us.

"Hurry, Yancy!" I said. "They're catching up!"

Yancy had longer legs than I did and I was pretty sure he could run faster than me on a normal day. And he could *definitely* run faster than me when I wasn't feeling well. At the same time, I knew carrying my weight was probably slowing him down.

"Look out!" I said.

Yancy tripped over a single block and we both took a spill. I hit the ground face first with a grunt and was just glad I didn't lose my grip on the crystal. When I opened my eyes, I saw the black feet of an Enderman hovering over me.

An arrow hit it, which I knew was Alex's doing. I whirled my head around to see Yancy stumbling to his feet. At the same time, Alex, Maison, Destiny, and Aunt Alexandra were racing toward us, taking out Endermen as they went. They knocked out one Enderman at a time here and there, but there was no way a small group could defeat this many on their own. In the far distance I could see other villagers rushing to help, but I knew they'd never make it in time.

"Come on, Yancy!" I shouted.

Then another Enderman was in front of us! Alex shot it with her arrow and Yancy and I ducked. We could almost see the cave from where we were! I thought maybe I was well enough to run, but I was wrong. I was even weaker than I thought, from the teleporting and from the fall. When I stumbled, Yancy caught me by the arm to steady me.

Two Endermen appeared in front of us, the rest close to our heels. My first thought was that Alex, who was keeping track behind us, would just knock out those two Endermen with her arrows. Then I saw that one of them was slightly shorter than the other. It was the last missing villager!

"Wait, Alex!" I shouted, in case she didn't notice the difference in all the chaos. From a distance they might all look the same size. It was only from up close that I could see the important difference. I threw myself at the shorter Enderman, trying to tap it with my purple crystal.

It disappeared. Alex hit the other Enderman.

No! I didn't know what to do. I couldn't lead the villager-Enderman down to the tunnel and risk destroying it with all the real Endermen! But I also couldn't risk myself and the Overworld by stopping to look for one villager, could I? As I kept running and looked around, I didn't see where it had teleported to.

"Yancy!" I called. "I saw the last villager! It's in this crowd!"

Yancy looked around wildly. "I don't see anything."

He wasn't the only one. Endermen were leaping and bolting behind us, appearing, disappearing. Looking back made me even more dizzy and slowed me down, so I had to look forward.

A small dot in the horizon caught my eyes. That little thing was the cave!

"Stevie! I found the villager!" I heard Maison call. She and the others were catching up, and she was pointing to an Enderman near her. Instead of striking it, she was trying to push it forward with her baseball bat, as if to push it toward me. In response, the Enderman hissed and lunged for her. This time she had to strike out with her baseball bat in self-defense, and the Enderman teleported away to safety. And it got lost in the crowd again.

Then I saw it, near me! It was to my side, so I had to stop running forward and go for it.

"Stevie, what . . . ?" Yancy cried, stopping in his tracks.

I vaulted toward the villager-Enderman. It disappeared and showed up a few feet away. The other Endermen were circling around me, the whole group of them closing in. This might be my only chance. It might be my worst decision too. But I had to try.

This time when I threw myself, I landed on the ground just in front of the villager-Enderman, my arm outstretched. It worked. The purple crystal touched its foot and everything turned violet.

I saw the transformation start to take place. It was so blinding I had to cover my eyes with my hand. In the violet haze there was an even more intense purple, and that belonged to the real Endermen's eyes. Those eyes looked even more crazed as they sensed their prey getting nearer. They were rushing at me against the purple backdrop, and in seconds they would overwhelm me.

Yancy jumped down beside me. The next second I was surrounded by Maison, Alex, and Destiny too, all of them holding their weapons out, surrounding me like a protective circle.

As the violet light went away, I knew even this circle wouldn't be enough.

We had only one chance now.

"Hold on to me!" I shouted, and threw the last Ender pearl toward the cave.

CHAPTER 24

I DIDN'T KNOW IF THIS WOULD EVEN WORK, BUT I felt everyone put their hands on my shoulders so we were connected. We were going to find out if an Ender pearl could teleport the five of us together.

The next few seconds were probably the worst of my life. Not only was there that awful, unable-to-breathe feeling, but I didn't know what would happen when I finished teleporting.

When I came to, I was even more tired and weak. I felt sore all over. I also noticed three things: I still had the precious crystal, we were closer to the cave now, and my friends were with me. They were all looking pretty dazed too, though not as much as I was.

The next thing I did was look behind me. The Ender pearl had thankfully given us some distance, though still not enough to feel relaxed at all. The

Endermen were swiftly moving across the field toward us. We were always thrown off when they teleported, but when we did the same trick, it didn't really give them any pause.

All five of us were on our feet and hurrying the final stretch to the cave. As I ran, my feet felt as if they weighed a thousand pounds. My side was split, ripping me with pain when I needed to run the fastest. This was the terrible cost of using those Ender pearls.

As we were running, listening to the hissing sound of the Endermen, everything felt like a blur. Was that the effect of the Ender pearl too? Everything was more intense and it seemed as if we were going in slow motion. The Endermen sounded even louder than before. I dared to look back behind us, and I saw that even though we were all running as fast as we could, we were losing our lead. Even after using our best defense, we might not make it to the cave in time. The Endermen were catching up, and we were weak and all out of Ender pearls to help us.

Even in all this craziness, I thought of something. I thought about the boy who was mocking me earlier and then who'd gotten turned into an Enderman after trying to be "a hero." He'd said he wanted glory. Maybe that was the difference. I didn't really feel I deserved to be called anything as great as a hero, and maybe that was because I never went out looking for glory. All the battles I'd been in had been self-defense, or fought to protect others. No, I definitely didn't go looking for danger. But if danger came my way, I wasn't about to hide and ignore it. I was going to risk everything for those I cared about.

The pain and fear made that all the more clear to me. Even though Maison, Yancy, and Destiny weren't from this world, they were willing to risk their lives too. Alex said she liked danger and adventure, but she was always there for a friend in need. They didn't put themselves in real danger for glory, but rather for friendship. For doing the right thing. And sometimes you had to face great odds and stand up to your biggest fears to do so.

Just as we reached the cave, the Endermen surrounded us.

CHAPTER 25

"WE'RE ALMOST THERE!" I SHOUTED. WE couldn't give up this close! I could even see the hole in the cave.

Endermen came up from behind us and then began teleporting in front of us. They had us surrounded.

"Just get down the hole!" Maison shouted. "We'll follow you!" She swung out her baseball bat, knocking it against an Enderman reaching out for me.

I felt bad for just running and not helping with the fighting, but I knew why Maison suggested this. We had to keep the crystal safe.

Staggering now, I came up on the hole. If only I didn't feel so dizzy. I pushed down the pain and kept going. I made myself concentrate on the hole so that I wouldn't be distracted by all the hissing behind me, by all the Endermen coming up to take us on.

Purple eyes appeared above me and I managed to duck in time for Destiny to take the Enderman out with her wooden sword. Now I was crawling, getting closer. As soon as the Enderman over me was gone, I stumbled back up and realized my knees were creaking.

I came up to the hole, my old enemy from earlier today. And, taking a deep breath, I plunged down into the darkness.

CHAPTER 26

I T TOOK A SECOND FOR MY EYES TO ADJUST. THE PUR-
ple glow of the crystal was the only thing lighting
my surroundings now. At first the tunnel looked
haunted with that eerie violet glow moving along the
walls.

The next thing I knew, I was surrounded.

As scary as seeing a pair of purple eyes in the darkness is, I still wasn't prepared to suddenly have a whole
mass of Endermen joining me. They'd teleported in
that instant. I swung my diamond sword at them, making them back off. Where were the others? Then Alex
landed behind me, her arrows at the ready. Maison was
next, followed by Yancy and Destiny.

"Run, Stevie!" Destiny called.

Putting my head down, I ran the best I could. Each
step seemed harder. I kept swinging my sword, keeping

the Endermen at bay. The others fought as backup, hitting all the Endermen they could get so that I could get through. Even with their help there was still an onslaught of enormous mobs in the way.

In the tunnel, everything felt more brutal. It was darker; it was closer together. The hisses of the Endermen were so close now that they rose up in a single, terrible roar. It was the kind of noise to fill your nightmares.

How much farther was the water?

I realized I couldn't remember exactly where it was. The tunnels all looked the same, and they were so confusing.

I was fighting mobs with one hand, and the other hand was trying to hold tightly to the purple crystal and touch the walls at the same time. I strained my ears, trying to hear the water on the other side. But the Endermen's hisses were were too loud for me to hear anything else.

Wall after wall was dry as a bone. Then finally my hand touched a block with dripping water.

"It's here!" I called out. I began hitting the block as fast and as hard as I could with my diamond sword. Now that I was standing in one place, the Endermen surrounded me again. They got in front of me so that I couldn't even reach the wall!

"I don't think so!" Maison said. She jumped in front of me, hitting the Endermen back. I remembered what made Maison and me such a good team, even before we started fighting our battles with the others. Maison cleared out the room for me and began banging the wall herself. I thrust my sword into it, and then I felt the wall crumble.

"Now!" I shouted, hoping the others could hear me.

I took a deep breath.

And the water came out and covered us all.

CHAPTER 27

THE PRESSURE OF THE WATER KNOCKED US ALL back. I was underwater and I opened my eyes. The purple crystal made the water tint violet just like everything else, and I could see the Endermen turning red and disappearing. Disappearing for real!

"You useless Endermen!" It was the evil voice again, blaring in my head. She was furious, watching her minions lose. *"You almost had it! I won't rest until I get that crystal!"*

And then the voice was gone, as if it had never been there.

In the mass of red Endermen, I glimpsed Maison swimming, her black hair floating all around her. Even though we'd defeated the mobs, there was no time to celebrate, because we were still in real danger of drowning. I could see Maison was scrambling in the direction of the hole we'd made in the wall, her arms and legs paddling. The pressure was so strong I could see she was also having trouble moving forward. The hole we'd opened up basically created its own waterfall and was flooding the entire area.

I swam in the direction of the hole. More and more Endermen vanished, clearing the water. Within seconds, they were all gone. It had been the right move to defeat them all at once. But now I was understanding why Dad was so worried. Swimming against this current would be challenging, especially while weak from teleporting with the Ender pearls.

It was starting to get harder to breathe. I tried to go up to the surface and I hit solid rock. No! The tunnel was completely full of water! I helplessly struck at the ceiling, as if I could push the blocks out of the way and breathe. It was no good. Then I knew the only chance I had was to get through the hole I'd just made, and hope there was air on the other side.

I could see where the opening was . . . it was just so difficult to get there. My arms were so tired I felt sick. My legs hurt.

And I needed to breathe. This was even worse than teleporting, because as scary as teleporting is, you know you're going to be able to breathe in a few seconds. You just had to hold on and wait it out.

I could see the air bubbles leaving my mouth and rising up. My lungs were screaming in pain as if they were going to burst. The more frantically I pushed myself, the closer I got to the opening, but it was only a little closer. It wasn't close enough for any relief. I didn't know if I had enough air to get me there.

In the *Minecraft* game they played on Earth, they showed the character's health with little hearts, and the more hearts on the screen, the healthier you were. I knew that if I were being looked at in the game, I had maybe a heart and a half left.

I felt something clamp down around my hand. There was Maison in front of me, her fingers curled around my blocky hand, pulling me forward with her. Her cheeks were puffed out and I knew she needed air too, but she saw I needed help even more. As she began to pull me with her, Alex showed up and grabbed my other hand. Then Yancy and Destiny were there, grabbing hold too. I felt myself start to move forward for real now, even with all the gushing water.

Together we pulled ourselves through the hole and into a dry area, gasping for breath, hardly able to believe we'd survived.

"We did it!" I said once I was able to catch my breath. I was so glad to be breathing again that the terror of the unknown voice fell to the background. "We really did it! The Endermen are gone!"

"See, this is what feels normal these days," Yancy wheezed. "If we're not all in terrible danger, it just feels boring."

"Oh, stop it, Yancy," Destiny said.

Then a hand came out of the hole and a large body pulled itself up beside us.

CHAPTER 28

MY FIRST THOUGHT WAS THAT A LONE ENDER-man had made it and was climbing up here to steal the crystal and get its revenge. But the body didn't have the long legs and arms. Or the purple eyes. It was Dad, who must have swum in from the tunnel's entrance.

"Dad!" I said, relieved.

The first thing Dad did was make sure we were all okay. Then he looked at the purple crystal, which I was still grasping in my hand.

"Amazing," Dad said.

"Did we take all of the Endermen out?" Alex bounced forward, wanting to know.

"There weren't any that I swam by," Dad said. "Alexandra is doing a final sweep of the area to see if any others are hiding around. Here." He reached into his toolkit and pulled out food for us. Wonderful food! I snatched the meat he gave me and swallowed it down almost without tasting it. All the pain from the attacks and Ender pearls vanished. I felt like new again. The others ate greedily too, though I don't know if they felt as much relief as I did!

"Good thing you know this tunnel so well, Stevie," Yancy remarked, stretching and taking another bite of cooked beef.

I felt embarrassed. Seeing my face, Maison said, "What? What's wrong?"

"I don't know this tunnel well," I blurted. "I fell down it earlier and an Enderman attacked me and I barely got out of here."

But I saw my friends were all smiling.

"The first Enderman I fought today was really hard too," Alex said. "You know, the one that appeared in my house? I wasn't sure if I was going to be able to beat it!"

Suddenly, I didn't know what I was so embarrassed about. These were my friends, and they weren't going to make fun of me for mistakes. Not like that mocking boy. Maybe we really could be the official Overworld Heroes, and help the villagers in times of need.

CHAPTER 29

WHEN WE CAME OUT OF THE TUNNEL AND back into the cave, there were crowds waiting for us. They were cheering.

"We checked the area, and no more Endermen were found!" Aunt Alexandra hooted with joy. To Dad, she said, "How could you doubt your big sister? When I form a group to save the Overworld, I know what I'm doing. The Overworld Heroes are going to make us proud again and again, you just wait. Maybe you and I could be a heroic task force too, if you weren't so stubborn."

"I'm not stubborn," Dad said. "You just argue with everything I do."

"I do not," Aunt Alexandra said.

"You just proved my point," Dad said.

"See, that's the stubborn thing," Aunt Alexandra

said. "You can't let anything be. Just be proud of your son, Steve. I'm proud of my daughter."

Now Dad looked my way. "I am proud of him," he said. "He just doesn't always listen. He can be a little . . ."

"Stubborn?" Aunt Alexandra said with a smile. "Gee, I wonder where he gets it from."

Someone cleared their throat loudly and I turned. It was a man I recognized but didn't know well, and he had his hand on the mocking boy's shoulder.

"Stevie," the man said. "I want to thank you. I was the person you changed back at the last minute, the one you stopped to help."

I realized it had been so crazy at that moment that I hadn't seen exactly who the villager had been. It was the mocking boy's dad!

"After my son went missing, my wife and I went looking for him," the man continued. "And the Endermen got me. But you saved me, and my son . . ." I could tell this was really emotional for him. Everyone else had turned and looked.

The mocking boy coughed awkwardly into his hand. "I'm, uh, sorry about earlier," he said. "For making fun of you and lying to your dad and stuff. I shouldn't have tried to be a hero."

I smiled and shook my head. "I never try to be a hero," I said. "I don't even think I deserve to be called that. I just do what I do to protect us all."

The boy looked at me as if he'd never thought of it that way. His eyes lit up.

"The Endermen are defeated," Aunt Alexandra said to Alex, Maison, Destiny, Yancy, and me. "Can I count on you five the next time something happens in the Overworld?"

I looked down at the purple crystal. "They're defeated *for now*," I corrected. "We still need to figure out what this crystal is. We need to protect it from the dark forces that might use it for harm. I have a feeling more mobs will be coming." I thought of the voice some of us had been hearing. Whatever that voice was, it and the crystal were linked, somehow. I just knew it.

"We'll get to the bottom of this mystery," Maison promised, looping her arm over my shoulders. "We won't let you down."

"Yeah, because we're the Overworld Heroes," Alex cut in.

"And we're going to do everything we can to live up to that name," I said. My hand closed tightly around the crystal as I remembered the voice I'd heard in the tunnel. Something evil was coming closer, but we had good on our side. "We won't let this crystal fall into the wrong hands. I swear it."

DO YOU LIKE FICTION FOR MINECRAFTERS?

Read the Unofficial Minecrafters Academy series!

Zombie Invasion
WINTER MORGAN

Skeleton Battle
WINTER MORGAN

Battle in the Overworld
WINTER MORGAN

Attack on Minecrafters Academy
WINTER MORGAN

Hidden in the Chest
WINTER MORGAN

Encounters in End City
WINTER MORGAN

Available wherever books are sold!